The House in the Forest

Written by Janet Foxley   Illustrated by Keino

 Collins

Chapter 1

"I'm still hungry," said Gretel. She looked longingly at the half loaf on the breakfast table.

"I'm *always* hungry," said Hansel. "Can't I have another slice of bread – just a thin one?"

"No," said their stepmother, "or there'll be nothing for supper." She quickly put the loaf in the cupboard, locked the door and slipped the key into her pocket. "It's time you were off to the forest."

Their real mother had died several years ago. The children hated calling their stepmother "Mum", so they used her name: Helga.

"The forest is dark and full of strange noises," said Gretel. "Can't you come with us, Dad?"

"Well …" Dad looked hopefully at Helga.

"Certainly not," she snapped. "You have to go to town to look for work again. If you haven't found a job by the end of today, there'll be trouble!"

Gretel shivered. She didn't like the way Helga said that. And they were in enough trouble already. If Dad didn't find a job soon, they'd be even hungrier – the firewood they gathered earned barely enough to buy a loaf.

3

"Perhaps they could stay at home today," said Dad. "It's so cold."

The first snow of winter had fallen in the night, and there was no money to replace the coats and boots the children had outgrown.

"If they don't gather firewood today," said Helga, "you'll have nothing to sell in the market tomorrow, and we'll have nothing to eat the day after that. Your children wouldn't have to work if *you* hadn't lost your tools."

Dad was a carpenter. He'd made desks for the head teacher, doors for the mayor and stairs for the king. But now he couldn't make anything for anyone, and the family had run out of money.

"Dad didn't *lose* his tools," Hansel protested. "They were *stolen*."

The children squeezed into their coats. Dad had only a scarf and hat – he'd sold *his* coat last week, to buy cheese.

Chapter 2

Dad set off for town with the bundle of firewood the children had collected the day before. He'd sell it in the market while he looked for a job.

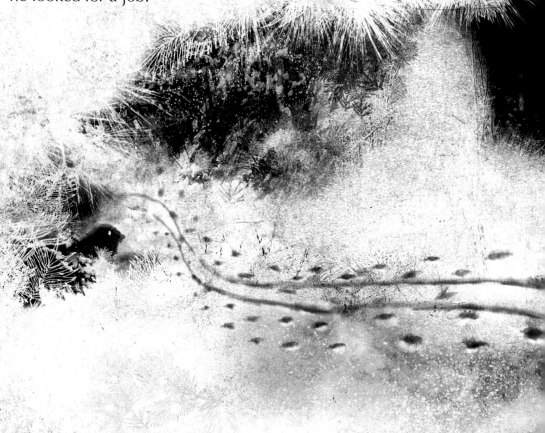

The children pushed their cart deep into the king's forest. Paths ran in all directions among the trees, and Gretel was afraid they'd get lost.

"Don't worry," said Hansel. "All we have to do is follow our footprints
in the snow and they'll lead us home."

Getting lost wasn't all Gretel was afraid of. She was scared
that every noise she heard was the footstep of a bear.
She was scared that every shadow that fell across the path
was a hungry wolf.

All day they worked hard gathering twigs and branches.
They noticed the noises and the shadows, but they didn't notice
it starting to snow again.

8

"I'm tired," Gretel said at last, "and it's getting dark. Let's go home."

"All right," said Hansel. "I'll just fetch this one last … *aaah!*"

"What's wrong?"

"Something's caught me. There are big teeth digging into my foot."

"Oh *no*! A wolf!"

"No – a trap. Go and fetch Dad. It *hurts*! Quick, Gretel, run!"

Gretel ran. The falling snow had covered their footprints, but she remembered which way they'd come.

Soon she came to a place where several paths met. And now she *couldn't* remember – all the paths looked alike. Tears welled up in her eyes, and snow melted on her hair and dripped down to join them. And then she saw a star twinkling through her tears.

Gretel wiped her eyes and looked again. It wasn't a star, but a lantern, lighting up the door of a cottage deep among the trees. She raced up to it and banged the door knocker.

The door opened a crack and
an old woman peered out.

"My brother's caught in a trap,"
Gretel said breathlessly.
"Can you help?"

"Your little brother," said the old
woman, "or your big brother?"

"My big brother." Gretel held up
her hand to show how tall
Hansel was.

The old woman grinned.
She hadn't many teeth left.
"Perfect," she muttered to herself
as she fetched her shawl
and walking stick.
"Big enough to work, but small
enough to slip through
a window."

Gretel was outside, and didn't
hear her.

12

The snow had covered her tracks again, but to Gretel's surprise, the old woman knew exactly where to find Hansel, who lay shivering and whimpering with pain.

"Out you come, young man," said the old woman, and she prised the jaws of the trap open with her walking stick.

Hansel crawled free. "I don't know how to thank you," he said, rubbing snow into his foot to dull the pain.

The old woman cackled. "Don't worry. *I* know exactly how you can thank me."

She helped Hansel to limp to her cottage and led them inside.

Chapter 3

The children gasped. Logs burnt in the grate, and by the light of the dancing flames they could see that the room was crammed with paintings and fine furniture, china and silver. There was even a glass case full of jewellery. The old woman was rich!

The old woman bandaged Hansel's foot. "Now you can start thanking me," she said, as soon as she'd finished.

"Knock this nail into the wall so I can hang my new painting." She gave him a hammer.

Hansel did it easily. It was just like using Dad's hammer.

"Now come outside and saw some logs for my fire." She gave him a saw.

Hansel did it easily. It was just like using Dad's saw. He carried the logs indoors.

The old woman grinned. "Just the right size of boy," she said. "I've lots more jobs you can thank me with."

There was something about her grin that frightened Gretel. "We must get home now," she said. "Dad'll be worried."

Hansel was beginning to feel frightened, too. "I'll come back tomorrow and do some more jobs for you," he said, and he grabbed Gretel's hand and headed for the door.

"Oh no, you won't!" screeched the old woman. "You're staying here." She grabbed Hansel and bundled him into a cupboard. Afraid she'd be next, Gretel did the first thing that came into her head. She picked up a heavy paperweight and dropped it on the floor. THUD!

The old woman spun round. "What was that?"

"I think there's a bear outside!" said Gretel, and she kicked
the paperweight so that it thudded again.

"More likely someone's stealing my logs." The old woman grabbed
her stick.

As soon as the old woman went to the door,
Gretel opened the cupboard and beckoned to Hansel
to come out, putting her finger to her lips to warn him
to be quiet. Hansel crept out and hid behind
the open cupboard door.

The old woman came back and saw the open door. "He's escaped!" she roared in fury.

"No, he hasn't," said Gretel. "He's right at the back, look."

The old woman took a step into the deep, dark cupboard.

Quick as a flash, Hansel slammed the door behind her and turned the key.

"Let's drag something heavy in front of the cupboard," he said, "in case she manages to break the lock."

"What about this tool box?" said Gretel. "It's very heavy, a bit like Dad's."

Hansel stared at it. He remembered the feel of the hammer in his hand. He remembered the feel of the saw in his hand. He whipped open the lid and looked inside.

"It *is* Dad's!" he said.

"*What?*" Gretel looked again at all the treasures in the room. "You mean all this is …"

"… stolen? Yes, it must be."

The old woman hammered on the cupboard door with her stick. "Just you wait!" she roared.

But waiting was the last thing the children wanted to do.

"Let's get out of here," said Hansel. "Quickly!"

They hurried out into the night.

"We're still lost," said Gretel. "We don't know which path leads home."

"Shh, listen, yes we do." In the distance the church clock was chiming midnight. "It's that way."

Hansel gathered up a pile of the old woman's logs.

"What are you doing?" asked Gretel.

"The snow will cover our footprints, but if we mark each turn we take with a log, we'll be able to tell the police the way to the cottage."

The children hurried back to the village.

Chapter 4

"Thank heavens you're safe," cried Dad, as they tumbled wearily through their cottage door. "I've been looking everywhere for you, but the snow had covered your tracks."

Gretel suddenly realised they'd left their cart of precious firewood in the forest.

"Where's Helga?" she asked nervously.

"Gone," sighed Dad. "When she said there'd be trouble, she meant she wasn't prepared to live on bread and water any longer. And it's bread and water again tonight, I'm afraid – I didn't find a job."

"You don't need one," cried Hansel, "we've found your tools!"

"And lots of other stolen things," said Gretel, and they explained excitedly.

Dad pulled on his boots. "I'm going to get the police," he said. "They must arrest that old woman at once."

Next morning, the news was all over the village. The old woman was arrested. Dad got his tools back and Hansel and Gretel were given 100 gold coins as a reward for finding the stolen property.

They were never cold or hungry again. And Helga can't have heard of their change of fortune, because she never came back.

FOREST NEWS

BRAVE CHILDREN TRAP THIEF

Two brave children, Hansel and Gretel, trapped a thief in her house in the forest at the weekend. The thief has now been arrested.

Hansel and Gretel were collecting firewood for their out-of-work dad. Disaster struck when they lost their way and Hansel got injured. Luckily an old woman who lived nearby helped them.

brave kids, Gretel and Hansel

But when they tried to leave, the woman shut Hansel in a cupboard! The children had to trick the old woman and lock her up instead. They ran home, marking the way with logs to lead the police back to the house.

the thief

inside the old woman's house

Gretel told police, "The house is crammed full of fine things – and as soon as we recognised our dad's tool box, we knew the old woman was a thief."

The old woman was arrested, the children were rewarded and their proud dad got his tool box back and returned to work as a carpenter.

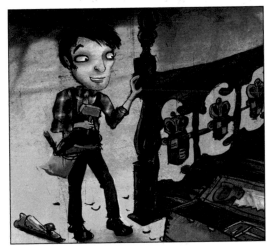

proud Dad back at work

Ideas for reading

Written by Linda Pagett B.Ed (hons), M.Ed
Lecturer and Educational Consultant

Learning objectives: infer characters' feelings in fiction; identify and make use of main points of text; clarify meaning through the use of speech marks; use some drama strategies to explore issues; spell using morphological rules

Curriculum links: Citizenship

Interest words: carpenter, footprints, lantern, prised, crammed, paperweight, cupboard, arrest, fortune

Resources: whiteboard, dictionary

Getting started

This book can be read over two or more reading sessions.

- Read the back cover together, drawing children's attention to the word *retelling* and discussing what it means.

- Encourage children to retell to each other the traditional story of Hansel and Gretel, using imaginative vocabulary.

- Decide and note together on the whiteboard which features of the traditional story the children expect to find in this story, e.g. wicked stepmother.

Reading and responding

- Browse through the pages, discussing the pictures and how they convey mood and atmosphere, prompting children where necessary.

- Turn to pp2–3 and draw children's attention to the speech marks. Explain that they are helpful in identifying dialogue. Demonstrate reading Chapter 1 with expression, using cues to help, e.g. italicised words have emphasis.

- Encourage children to read silently and independently to the end of the book. Support weaker readers by hearing them read, prompting and praising.

- Remind children to read for meaning when they come across difficult words, asking themselves *does this make sense?*